THIS BOOK BELONGS TO

children's choice®

A Children's Choice® Book Club Edition from Macmillan Book Clubs, Inc.

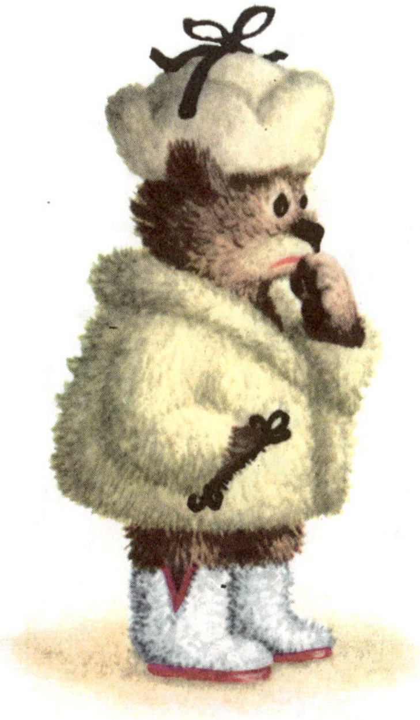

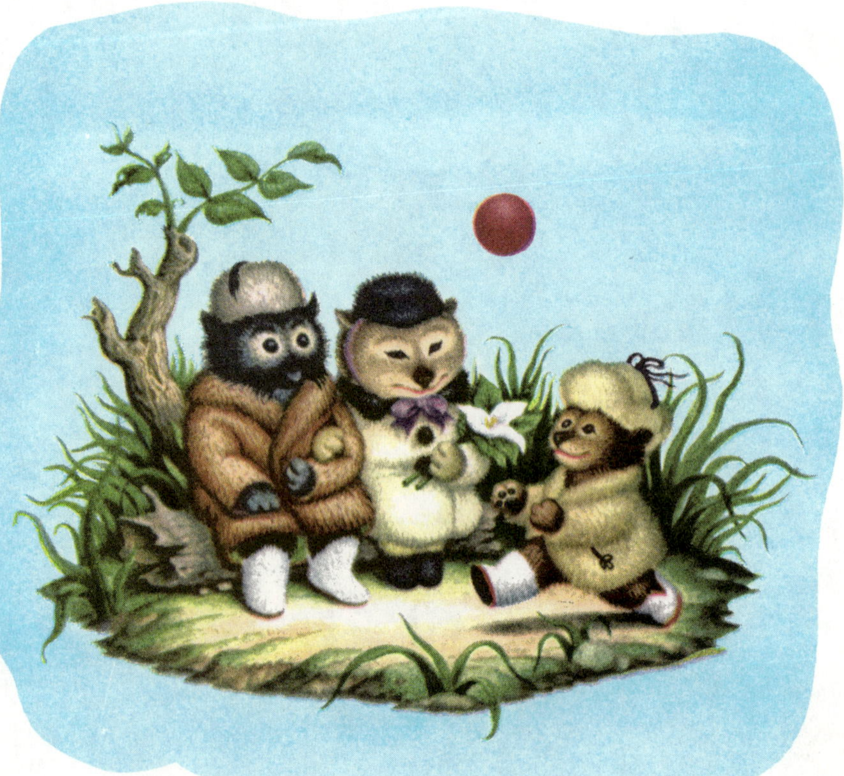

LITTLE FUR FAMILY

STORY BY

MARGARET WISE BROWN

PICTURES BY

GARTH WILLIAMS

COPYRIGHT, 1946, BY
HARPER & ROW, PUBLISHERS, NEW YORK AND EVANSTON

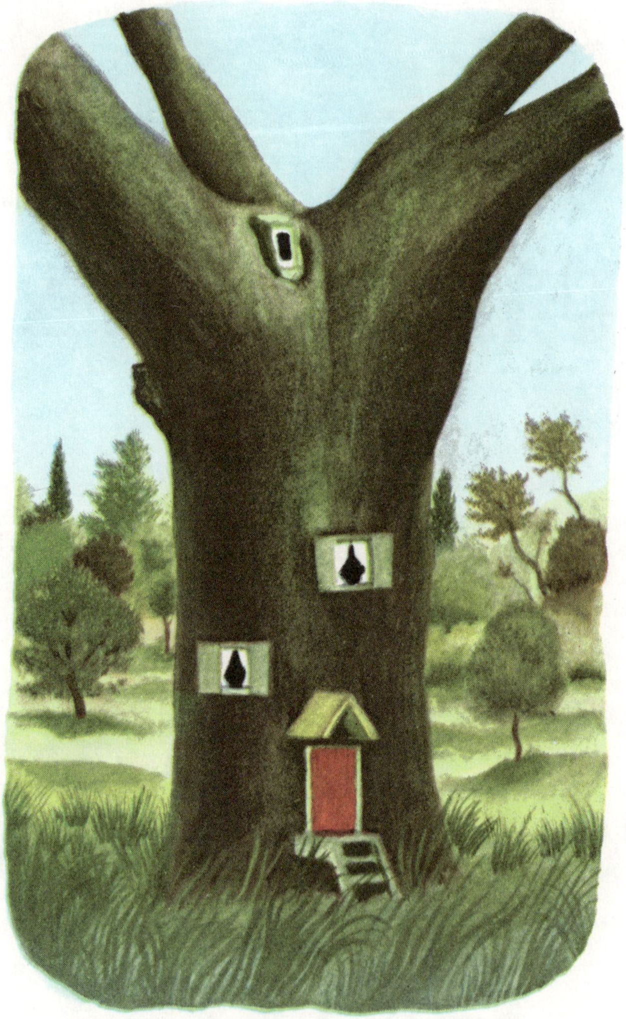

There was a little fur family
warm as toast
smaller than most
in little fur coats
and they lived in a warm wooden tree.

The little fur father
said good morning one day
put on his hat and went away
out into his little fur world.

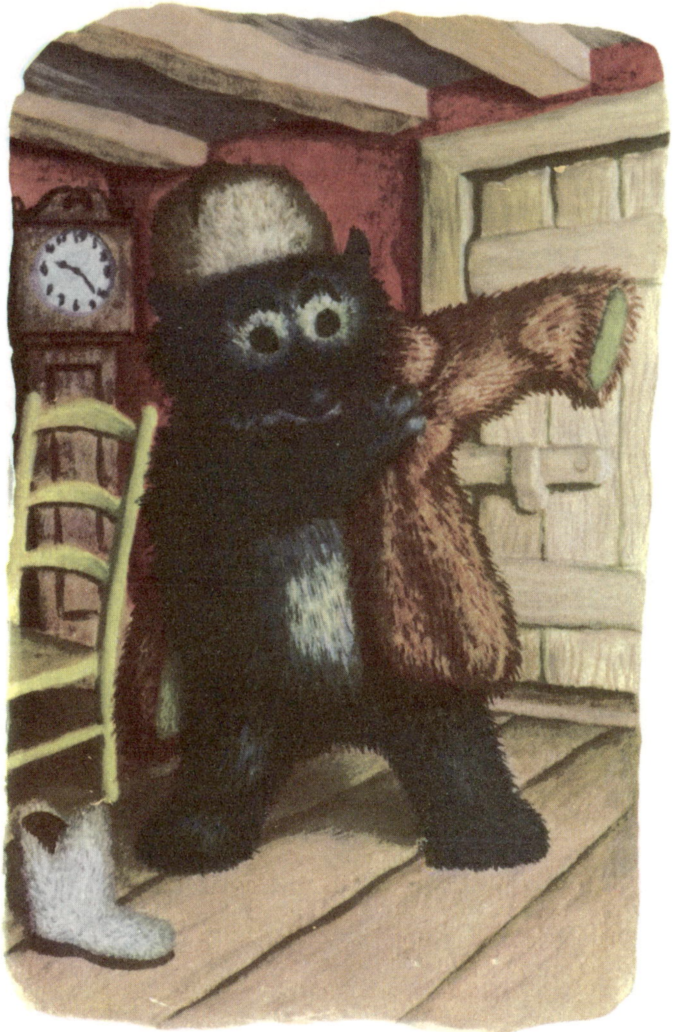

The little fur mother
bathed her fur child

and off he went
to play in the wild wood
where they lived.

It was a wild wild wood.
Wild flowers grew all over the ground
and wild winds blew through the air.
Wild nuts fell from the wild nut trees
and wild grass tickled the fur child's nose,
tickled his nose and made him sneeze. . . .
  Kerchoo!

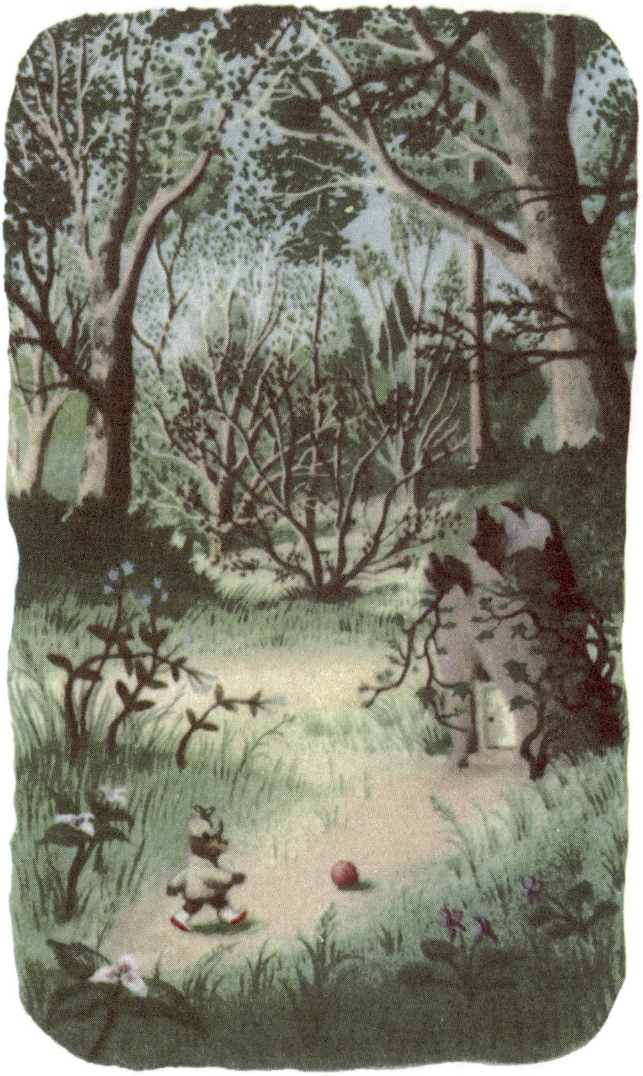

Kerchoo!

That sneeze woke up his grandpa
who lived in a hollow stump
and grandpa came walking
   thump thump thump
and walked out of his hollow stump
   and said—"Bless you
my little fur grandson.
Everytime you sneeze. . . .

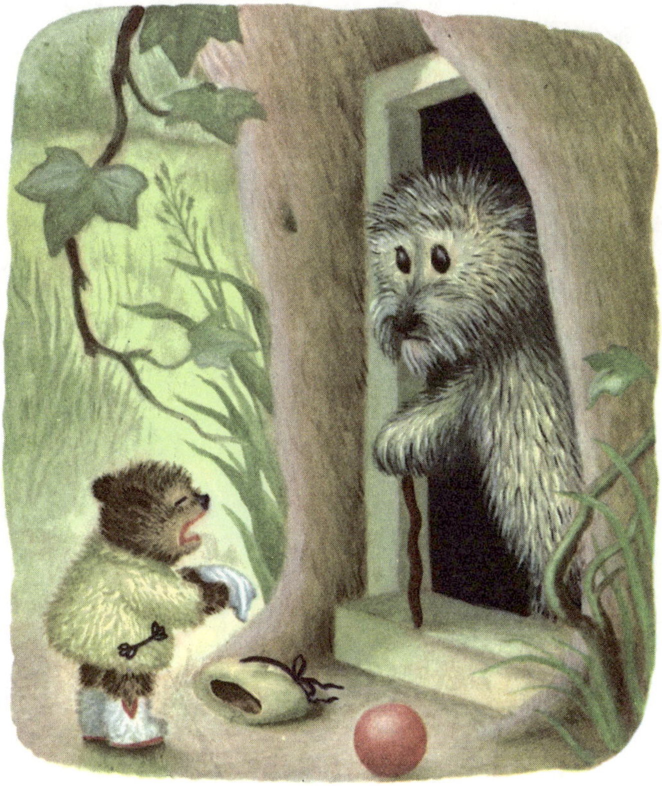

Kerchoo!"

"Bless you" said the little fur child.

"Thank you" said his grandpa.
Then old grandpa went
   thump thump thump
and walked back into his hollow stump.
And the fur child went on
through the dark and sunny woods
till he came to a
little river full of fish.

The fish didn't have any fur
and they didn't have any feet
and they swam around

under the river.
The little fur child watched
them for a long time.

Then, he reached in the river
and pulled out a fish
and looked at it
and then, *Kerplunk!*
He threw it back in the river.

He reached into the air
and he caught a flying bug
and he held it in his hand
and he looked at it.

The bug didn't have any fur.
It was shiny and had little wings.
Then————*ssip*
He threw it back in the air.

Then he caught a little tiny tiny fur animal
The littlest fur animal in the world.
It had warm silky fur and
   even a little fur nose.
So he kissed it right on its little fur nose
and put it gently back in the grass

and the little tiny tiny fur animal
ran down a hole into the ground.

The sun went down
beyond the river.
The sky grew wild and red
and the little fur child
turned around and
ran for home.

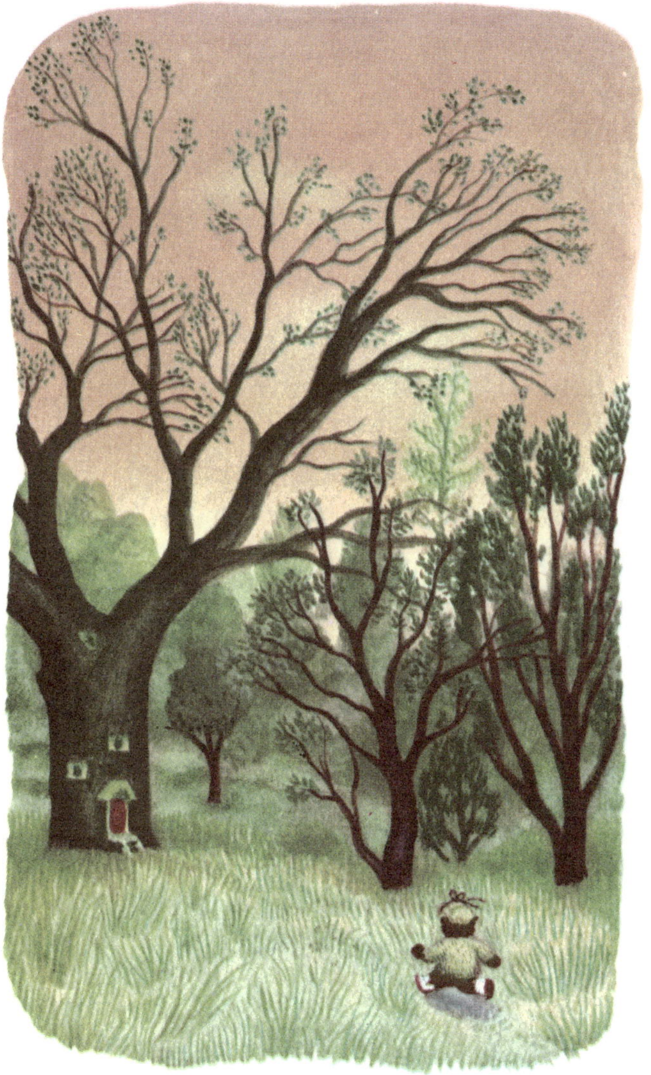

And just as the darkness got very dark
he bumped into his big fur mother
and she took her little fur child
home in her arms
and gave him his supper.

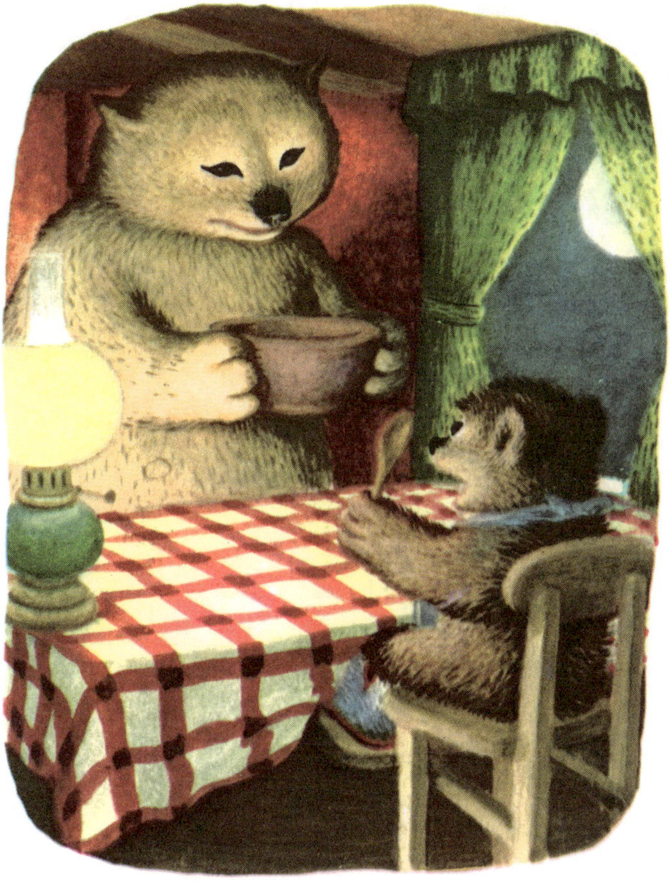

And there was his father
who put him to bed
and they tucked him in bed
all soft and all warm

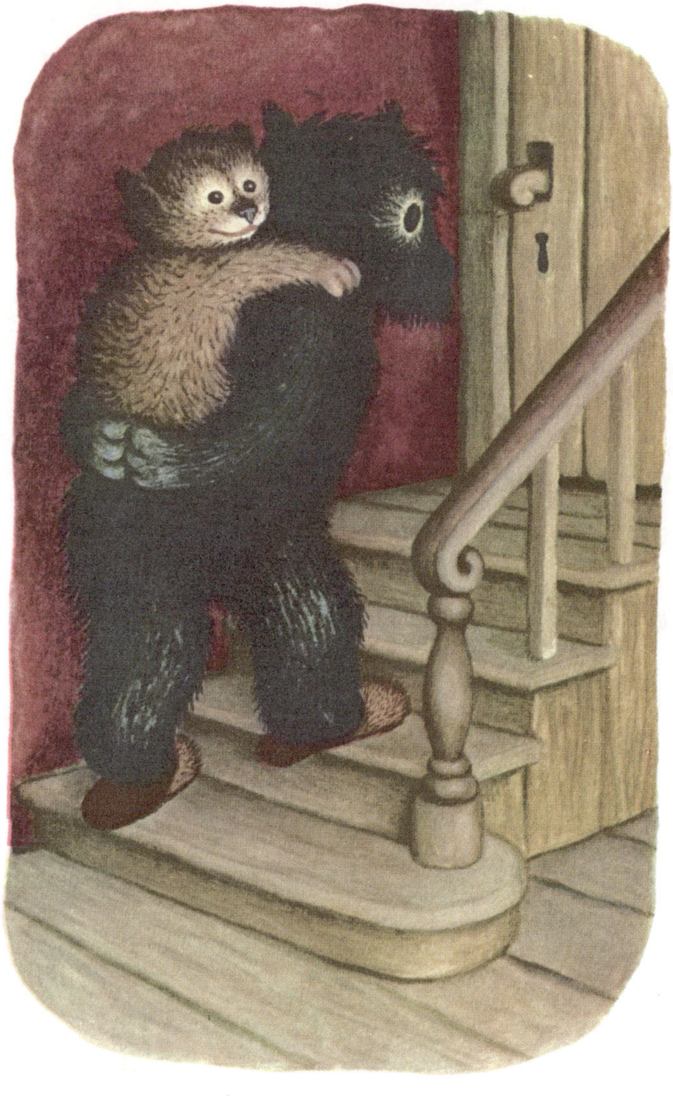

and they held his paw
and they sang him a song.

*Sleep, sleep, our little fur child,
Out of the windiness,
Out of the wild.
Sleep warm in your fur
All night long,
In your little fur family.
This is a song.*

THE END

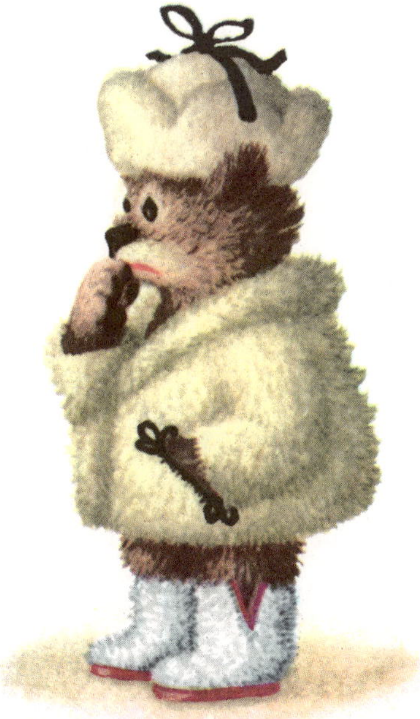

Macmillan Book Clubs, Inc. offers a wide variety of products for children. For details on ordering, please write Macmillan Book Clubs, Inc., 6 Commercial Street, Hicksville, N.Y. 11801.